ON TUMBLEDOWN HILL

By Tim Wynne-Jones
Illustrated by Dušan Petričić

To the merry gang
who attended "summer camp"
at Red Deer College 1988–1993,
friends and colleagues one and all
–T. W-J.

For Caca and Branko,
friends you would like to have
–D.P.

NORTHERN
LIGHTS BOOKS FOR CHILDREN

Red Deer College Press

Tim Wynne-Jones

ON
TUMBLEDOWN HILL

Illustrated by
Dušan Petričić

Northern Lights Books for Children are published by
Red Deer College Press
56 Avenue & 32 Street Box 5005
Red Deer Alberta Canada T4N 5H5

Acknowledgments
Edited by Peter Carver
Cover design by Kunz + Associates
Art direction and text design by Dušan Petričić
Printed and bound in Hong Kong for Red Deer College Press

5 4 3 2 1

Financial support provided by the Alberta Foundation for the Arts, a benefi-
ciary of the Lottery Fund of the Government of Alberta, and by the Canada
Council, the Department of Canadian Heritage and Red Deer College.

COMMITTED TO THE DEVELOPMENT OF CULTURE AND THE ARTS

Canadian Cataloguing in Publication Data

Wynne-Jones, Tim.
On Tumbledown Hill
(Northern lights books for children)
ISBN 0-88995-186-1
I. Petričić, Dušan. II. Title. III. Series.
PS8595.Y59O6 1998   jC813'.54   C98-910479-6
PZ7.W993On 1998

There are twenty-six monsters, all much bigger than me and stronger, too, with arms that are longer and thicker through, standing like trees on Tumbledown Hill!

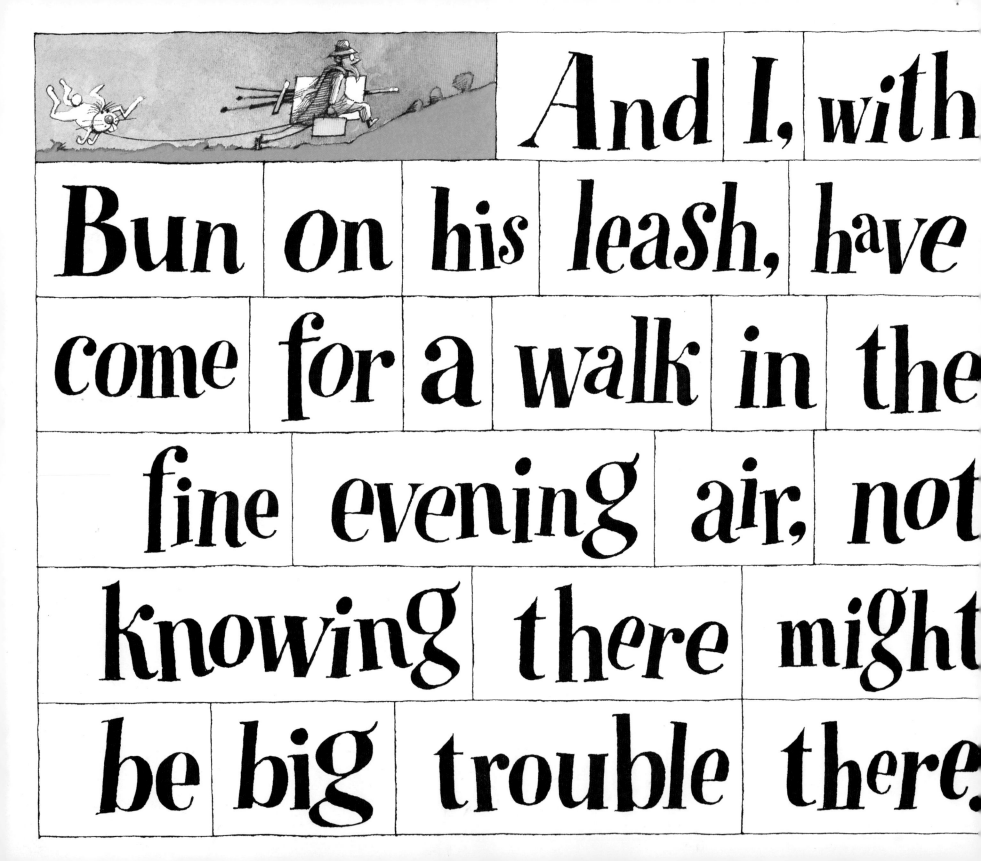

And I, with Bun on his leash, have come for a walk in the fine evening air, not knowing there might be big trouble there.

Bun likes the clover and I like the view on Tumbledown Hill, so we nibble and scribble 'til we've both had our fill.

Then out of the blue and to my great dread, a boulder sails by as 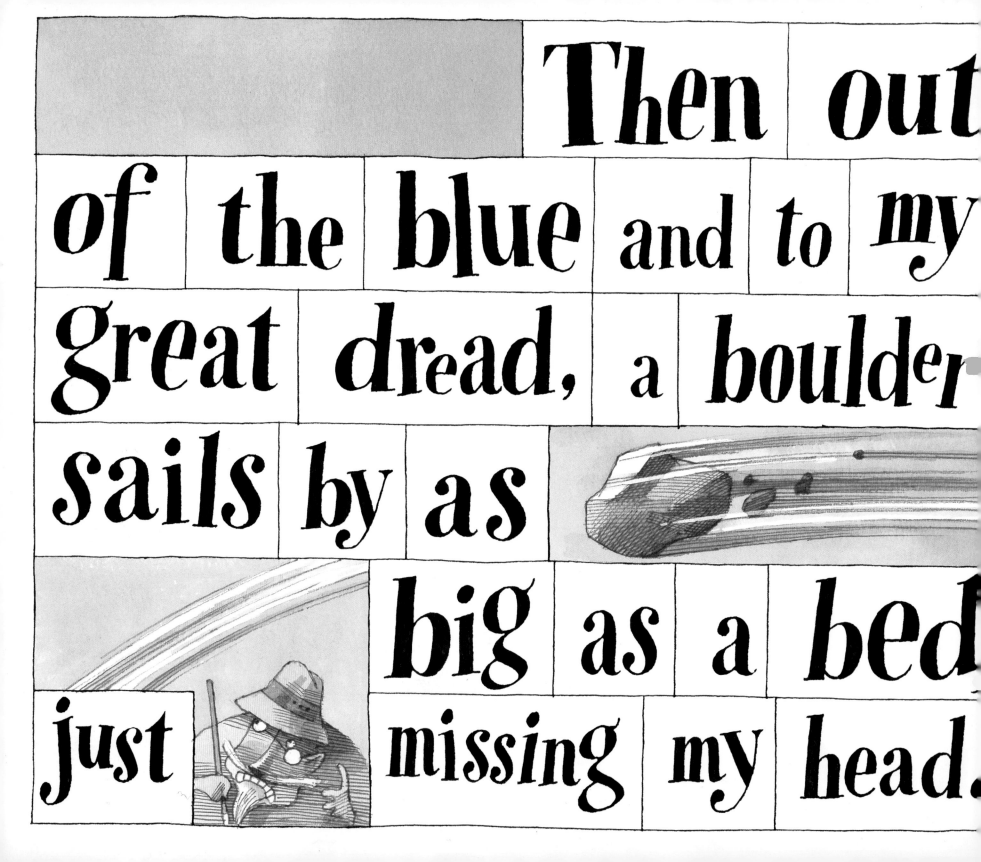 big as a bed just missing my head.

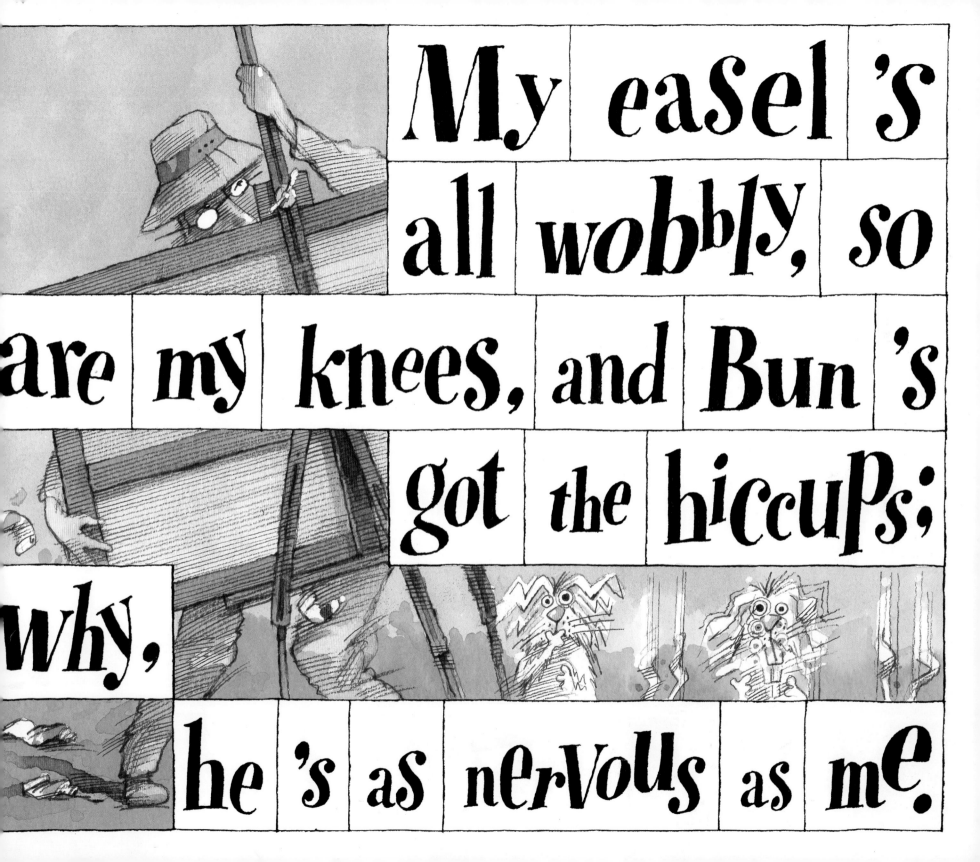

Oh, twenty-six monsters sure get in the way when you're trying to paint and all they want is to play.

One draws on the sidewalk, two more start a fight, three leap in the fountain and four ride a bike.

Five monsters blow bubbles, six roll on the ground, and those that are left kick a tin can around.

They scratch up their elbows and scrape up their knees and splash themselves silly, just as they please.

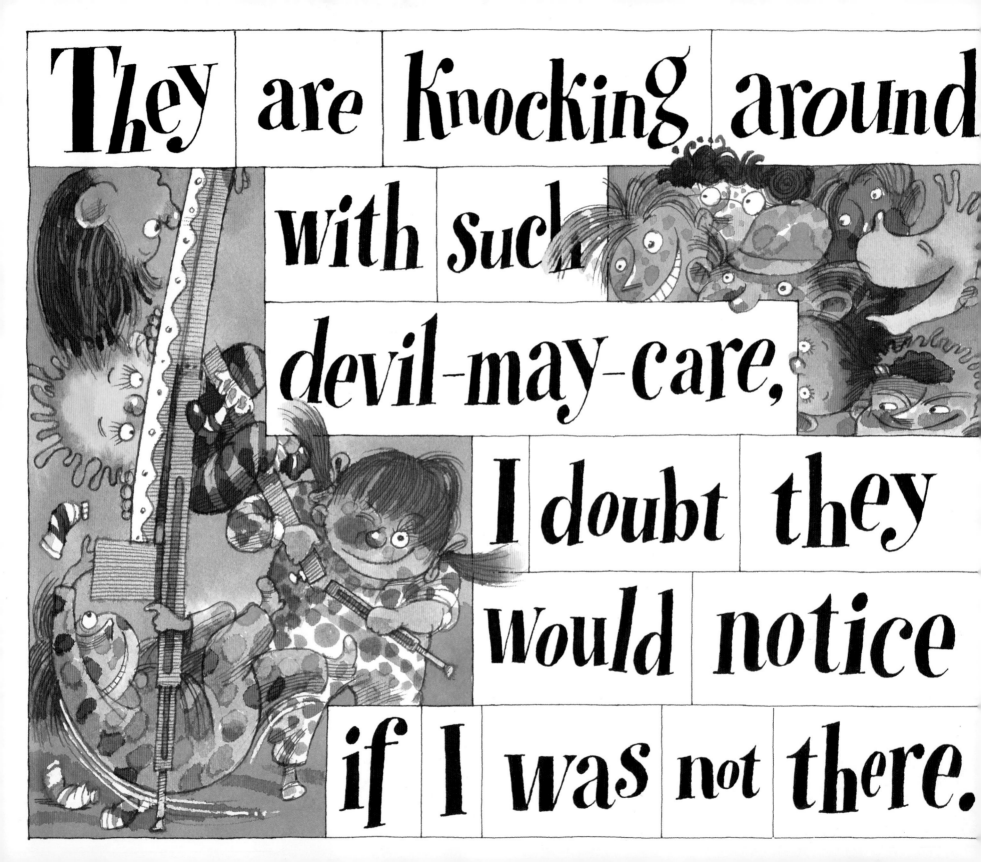

They are knocking around with such devil-may-care, I doubt they would notice if I was not there.

Yes, leaving seems prudent, sensible, good, and I doubt they would notice, but maybe they would.

And maybe they'd chase me just for the thrill, around and around Tumbledown Hill.

So it's best not to move and it's best just to paint.

It's much better to paint when you're scared than to faint.

And it's good when scared not to do too much thinking.

There's work to be done and the sun is sinking.

So I paint these monsters right out of my head.

Vamoosed, skedaddled, they've cleared out of town.

ON TUMBLEDOWN HILL

Twenty-Six to One

A story in twenty-six sentences—no more!
And every sentence is one word shorter
than the sentence before.
  by Tim Wynne-Jones

Note: Contractions counts as two words.
Hyphenated words count as one.

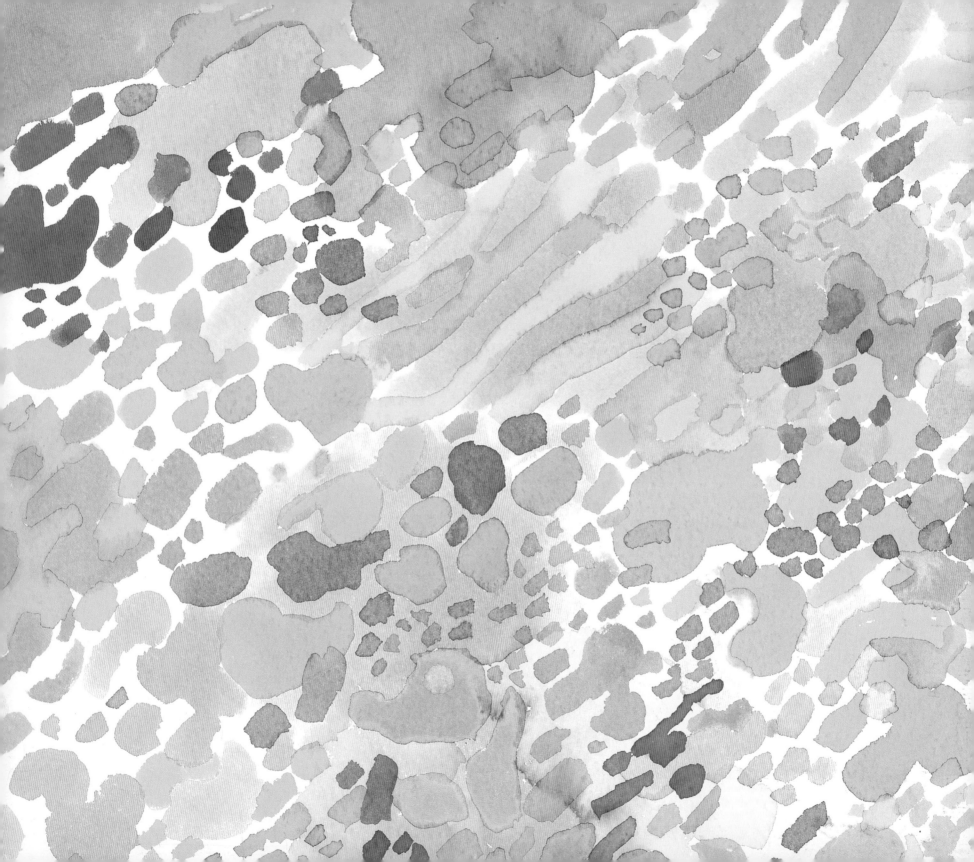